Table of Contents

.... 1

About the Adult FairyTales Book Series.................................. 3

Short Story 1: Only Me.. 5

Short Story 2: Knights of Faith 13

Short Story 3: The Chest 19

Short Story 4: The Old Man and the Forest 25

Short Story 5: The Call.. 31

Short Story 6: Teddy Bears 37

Short Story 7: Romphaea...43

Short Story 8: Darkness 49

Short Story 9: Temporal Paradox.....................................59

Short Story 10: Gülek's Pine Tree 65

About James Antoniou.. 71

Connect with James Antoniou.. 73

2

---

1. https://eculthub.blogspot.com/

2. https://eculthub.blogspot.com/

About the Adult FairyTales Book Series

Staying faithful, in the promise we made to provide free trips to the sphere of imagination, we decided to start a weekly series of short stories, through my personal blog.

In short, we presented a short story every Friday, during last winter, which all made this book (plus extra new stories).

Wanting to get closer to my personal favorite writing style, the stories are Adult Fairytales. I mean that they are short fairy-tales for adults, which increasingly approach horror, with a more "fairy-tallish" narrative complexion.

I wanted also to thank you, for receiving your comments and your ideas about where you would like the next story to travel your imagination, a fact that helped me build the new stories.

Kindly,
your "fairy-tale storyteller"
James Antoniou

Short Story 1: Only Me

10 years ago

The air smells like summer, even though it is already November. Inside a bus, a mother and her little boy are looking at the street. The mother's name is Aspasia. She is a young, sweet woman, which lives and breathes for the boy sitting next to her. Anestis is her first child and the first grandchild in her family.

The little boy began complaining two or three days ago, about a pain in his belly. Aspasia made him a few hot soups, but there was no improvement. Last night, while being sleepless for the third night in a row, her husband suggested that it would be a good idea, to get the child to a doctor.

It was almost eleven, when mother and son crossed the door of the hospital. The doctor was an old acquaintance of the family. He was well over sixty and had also been Aspasia's doctor when she was a child. After examining the child, he called her in his office and told her that the boy has appendicitis and should be operated immediately. The young woman felt her legs trembling and the room's lights shimmering.

"Don't be afraid" said the doctor, "it's nothing but a simple routine surgery. Tomorrow you'll both be home, as if nothing ever happened".

Aspasia spoke on the phone with her husband, who was clearly calmer. He told her not to worry and that he would immediately leave his job and meet them in the hospital. Half an hour later, the nurses prepared the kid and passed through the doors, leading to the surgery rooms. Aspasia bent down and kissed her son gently on the cheek. Before the warm, metallic taste of the hypnotic gas wrap him into oblivion, the boy turned his face towards his mother.

"Mommy, do you love me?" he asked her.

"I love you more than you can imagine" she replied.

"Mommy, am I your only love?"

"You are my one and only love, sweetheart; you will be my one and only love forever".

The boy's eyes closed and the stretcher was lost to the depth of the corridor.

3 days ago

His eyes open. Light, hot and bright light. It blinds him. His eyes are burning. The last thing he remembers is the stretcher of a hospital. The last image he has is the face of his mother. Where is she now? Why has she left him alone? He tries to shout; nothing but silence. He tries to run; he cannot move. He lowers his gaze; emptiness. He looks up; total emptiness. How is it possible to be standing on nothing and not fall?

"Where is my mother? Why am I alone?"

He hears someone calling him. The sound reminds him of his mother's voice. Where is the sound coming from?

"Mommy, where are you?"

He is starting to get scared. After all, why shouldn't he be afraid? He is only eight years old. He has every right to be scared, to cry, or to do whatever he wants to... He does not want to cry. Something has changed. He does not feel like a child anymore.

His mother's voice is still echoing. Not from somewhere around him, but from within him. The voice comes from inside his mind; from the depths of his soul. He closes his eyes and tries to figure out where the voice is coming from. He feels like being pulled and repelled at the same time. He opens his eyes... It's unbelievable.

He is standing outside a beautiful house. It's clean and freshly colored. It also has a swing and a very beautiful fountain. The wind blows loudly. The child approaches the house. He goes through the door without understanding how. He may not remember how he entered, but he is in the house.

In the living room, a woman is looking out of the balcony door. He calls her, but she does not hear him. Now, he shouts. The woman gets scared. She is old but looks amazingly like his mom. She is not his mom though; she is older and has a baby. Why is she terrified? What happened to her?

He talks to her, trying to calm her down.

"Don't be afraid, I am just a child. I can't hurt you."

The woman grabs the baby and runs around the house scared. He gets scared once more. He closes his eyes, trying to avoid seeing her. He hates seeing her so scared.

He opens his eyes again. He stands at exactly the same spot but the woman that looks like his mom, is gone. He shouts; he cries. He wants to leave, but he can't. He closes his eyes. He does not want to open them. He wants his mother. He calls her. No reply. His eyes close again.

Deep within, he knows that he does not want to keep his eyes closed, because he can't see around and that is scaring him. What will happen if he opens them, though? What will he see? With as much courage as an eight-year-old child can have, he slowly opens his eyelids.

The woman sleeps on the couch. Next to her, the baby lays; it's very small, tiny.

"That's how all mothers should be" he thinks. "They have to keep their children close to them, not like mine who has left me alone for so long."

He looks around and sees some photos. He picks them up with his hands and looks at them. It is him and mom. A smile of relief starts forming on his lips.

"Since they have our photos, they must be mom's friends. Mommy probably went somewhere around here and will soon be back."

A man is coming down the ladder. The boy knows him, has seen him in his dreams. He passes behind the table, next to the woman and then, grabs the pictures and looks at them.

"No Sir, don't touch them, they are ours" says the boy.

The man puts the photos back on the table.

"They are ours!"

The man enters the kitchen and the little boy immediately goes over them. How beautiful mommy is, in these photos.

A hand passes through him.

"How... I must be dreaming!" the boy thinks.

The man standing behind him, passes his hand once more through his back, pulls back the photos and throws them into a drawer.

"How did this happen;"

His little heart is about to break.

The man asks the woman who the boy in the photo is. He calls her Aspasia. That is his mother's name! His wife replies that she had a son with her ex-husband, which died at the age of eight. The man, very irritated, asks her how on earth after six years of marriage, she never told him that she had a child with her ex-husband, and above all, why on earth she never told him that the child had died.

"I am not dead" says the boy, "I am right here and you are too old to be my mother."

At the same time, a huge wave clears his mind.

Suddenly, the boy understands...

2 days ago

It's dawn. The light is trying to consolidate its dominance in the realm of darkness. The air is blowing really hard. It is not cold, but the moisture feels like a razor. At a corner of the garden, a man is seated on a bench.

He has his arms wrapped around his frozen body. He is not trying to warm up; he does not feel the cold. His mind is running away. A few hours ago, he raised his voice to his wife for the first time in his life. The worst part is that he raised his voice in front of their baby. He wonders why Aspasia had never told him about her dead child. They are together for almost seven years. The man had been sitting on the bench since then, almost all night.

He does not understand why things went wrong. Why does he feel so angry? Probably, the problem is that he is not sleeping well. But how could he sleep? Every night he sees the same dream.

In his dream, he is walking inside the house, which is their own, but at the same time, the furniture is completely different. It feels like someone else is living in their own home. He sees that he goes downstairs, in the living room. In an armchair with her back turned to him, a woman is siting. She is beautiful. She wears her long black hair over her head and a soft white dress, open on the shoulders.

He goes behind her. He approaches her. Her neck is white and looks incredibly soft. Thin hair covers her backbone. He wants to touch her. He stretches his hands. His left hand leans on her shoulder and goes up to her neck. The woman shudders. His right hand is approaching slowly towards her neck. He is holding a gun. The gun approaches the woman's neck. He feels his finger touching the trigger, tightening. He tries to stop it, but he cannot. Sweat drips on his forehead and enters his eyes. His eyes hurt him. At this point, he always wakes up.

"I can't take it anymore" he thinks. "I haven't closed my eyes for three days".

Until now, he thought that the nightmares were caused by the books he reads and he is simply being affected. Since yesterday though, he feels scared. He is afraid of himself and the dreams he sees. He is afraid for his wife. He is afraid for his child. His anger alienates him from the people he loves; makes him distant and bad. He has to find a way to calm down, for the sake of his family. His gaze gets lost in the forest, behind the house. Out here, everything looks so peaceful. The man lies on the bench and falls asleep.

3 days ago

After understanding, the pain came. The little boy had to accept that he was dead. But how could he be dead, since he is here? He can see, he can hear. He is alive, feeling.

On the other hand, if he was dead, why on earth is he here after all those years? Thinking how much his mother has grown up, he must have been dead at least for five to ten years. Why is he back? What brought him back?

The boy stands over his mother's head and looks at the baby. The baby's hair is sticking on his forehead.

"He probably feels hot" he thinks and stretches his hand to pull the hair off.

He can't touch the baby. His hands penetrate the baby's head, as if the baby was made just from air. The boy bends his head.

"What is the meaning of being here, if I can't even do the simplest things", the boy wonders.

A moment later, a soft cry pulls him out of his thoughts. He raises his head and looks at the baby. Two huge eyes are looking at him and a sweet smile flickers on the baby's face.

"The baby can see me. Oh my God, the baby can see me!" says the boy.

He starts making faces, playing with his hands. The baby turns all his attention on him and starts to laugh.

Once, his mother had told him that babies can see angels, because they have virtuous souls and that angels are there to protect them from evil.

"Is that why I came back?" the boy wonders. "Maybe I am an angel. But why hasn't my angel protected me? Why did he let me die?"

As if listening to his thoughts, the baby stops smiling and scared, starts whimpering. At the door of the bedroom, his father appears. The man walks to the bed and takes the baby in his arms. The baby stops crying. His mother turns around on the bed and hugs the man and the baby, smiling.

The beautiful image causes something inside the child to break. His mind goes back to his own father, holding him in his arms. He remembers his mother smiling happily. He turns his gaze to the man, who tacks the baby in and lies down beside them.

Today

Outside the house everything is peaceful. All one could hear is the wind that sighs as it passes between the leaves of the trees and the swing moving gently. Aspasia is sitting on an armchair, watching TV. Her head is placed on a pillow and she is taking a nap. She does not hear the steps descending the ladder behind her. Her husband reaches the last step and stops, looking at the edge of her neck. He looks hypnotized.

White skin and thin hair cover her neck. Her husband approaches her and touches her neck with his hand. He caresses her. Aspasia gives a soft gurgle of pleasure. His other hand approaches her. He is holding something; something made of metal, shining from the light of the TV set. The sound of a dripping tap is heard from the kitchen.

If the woman could see, she would see her first child's spirit, moving behind her husband. She would see a black shadow overflowing the boy's body. The man touches the bright metallic object on her neck and presses it. Thick, red blood dyes the base of her throat and her t-shirt. The man as if awakening from lethargy, understands what he just did and throws the knife on the floor. The child's spirit looks at the knife falling and smiles.

The man runs out of the house, screaming. A car is approaching the house at high speed. The knife reaches the floor and stops. The car hits the man and throws him to the side. His head hits the corner of the pavement.

"You said that I am your one and only love; that I will be your one and only love, forever".

Short Story 2: Knights of Faith

You could say he that did not like the company of people. Some would say that he was almost a misanthropist. Others would only say that he wanted his peace. Peter lived in Greece for many years. No one knew when he came to Kaisariani or where he came from. His was handling Greek very well but his accent was a little weird, he sounded more like talking in ancient Greek. He lived alone with an ugly dog in a room on the roof of a block of flats. The neighborhood could see him leave late at night and come back at dawn. Everyone assumed that he probably was working as a night-watchman or in a nightclub.

You could not call him a bad person. He never had any fights, he was just quite. He was buying everything he needed from the neighborhood' shops and was lost again in his home, until the night, when was beginning like always to walk up the road going to the mountain of Hymettus. His steps were always heavy and he carried a backpack. Next to him, his ugly dog was always walking.

The only person whose company he seemed to enjoy was the son of Father Hieronymus, the priest of the local church. A twenty-five-year-old man called Petros. You could often see them sitting in the courtyard of the church, like two people knowing each other very well. The young man had a huge body and was known for his gentle character and his tendency to warmly help anyone who needed him.

Some of the neighbors began to make bitter comments about their friendship, but because of his father who was a priest, or perhaps because of the moral character of the young man, they stopped almost right away. In the cessation of these comments also contributed greatly, the young man's long-term relationship with a girl who was absorbing most of his time. The real nature of Petros' and Peter's relationship appeared after some time, the summer when everything began.

It was almost August and the weather was really hot. The entire neighborhood was sitting all evening either on the balconies or on the sidewalk, since it was almost impossible to sleep. They had seen Peter leaving like always, going up the mountain. It must have been close to one after midnight, when the earth began to tremble. Screams of terror and fuss covered the old neighborhood. All people where terrified, every house in the neighborhood was ready to collapse. The tremble of the earth didn't last long, but it seemed to everyone that it took hours to stop.

Of course, the whole neighborhood stayed on the sidewalk and in the cars, so when Peter returned home, everyone saw him. The man seemed to have come out of hell. His face and hands were covered with dust and full of scratches and dried blood. His clothes dirty and ripped in many places and for the first time, he was not accompanied by his dog. The man walked to the door of his house and suddenly, knelt down on the stairs. Some people ran to help him, but with one move of his hand, he showed them that he was ok. He got up and bumped into the depth of the entrance. A few minutes later, Father Ierotheos and his son arrived. They passed through the open door and climbed the stairs to Peter's house. After a while, all three of them came down and started running up the road to the mountain.

Shortly before they reached the mountain, Petros left them. The two men continued running towards an old chapel on the mountain. The moment they reached its door, they saw dark shapes in the light of the candles. In front of their weak glow, moving pieces of darkness were visible.

The creatures that lived in the bosom of the Earth, once again had made their way out. They once again were trying to conquer the sunny world of the surface. The creatures with the thousand names, throughout time, threatened once more our world. Those called shadow people, gnomes, goblins, black-dawrfs, ogres, trolls, yaoguai and other names, in every part of the world, were coming back to the surface after almost a hundred years.

Peter, stepped in, opened his backpack and pulled out a sparkling sword. Father Ierotheos pulled the big cross he wore around his throat and removing his bottom, revealed a well-cut dagger. Then, together, as a man, they moved toward the shadows. Perhaps, if they could kill the ones they could see, they could break their way out.

As long as the monsters were forced to come out of the narrow hole, under the sanctuary of the church, the two men could, once they were able to fight a monster at a time, slaughter them before they could make a larger number. If they did not, the end of two men, the end of two Knights of Faith, and perhaps the end of the human race would come.

Young Petros had not come with them in the chapel; he had left to alert the rest of the Knights of the Battalion. The two men had to endure until the aid would come. They had to keep the monsters under the Earth, to retain them in the dark, where they belonged.

Their task was not easy and after some time, it would become more difficult. They were just two men, trained in battle, but fatigue would finally put them down.

Both the Priest and Peter took places left and right from the entrance of the hole, and slashed the creatures as they appeared. They had already killed all that made their way out, or at least they thought so. They could not be sure. These inconceivable creatures were one with darkness. There was no way to know if there was one hiding somewhere, until its sharp nails or dirty teeth protruding from its mouth and covering almost the underside of its ugly face, would hit their bodies.

Everything seemed to go well. The two Knights had managed to temporarily suspend the first wave of monsters. Now, they were simply listening to the grunts and their rudimentary language of communication deep inside the earth. They could, at last, take a breath.

Father Ierotheos gasping smiled to Peter.

"I think we made it", he said.

Peter looked at the Priest's face in the dim light of the church candles and suddenly, froze. A long and thin hand with sharp, dark nails grabbed his neck. The Priest immediately spread his hand and pushed the dagger he held in the dim eye of the monster.Peter and the monster collapsed at the same instant. The last move of the monster before dying was to clamp his fingers, forbidding the air to pass through the lungs of the knight. The Priest tried to untie the monster's fingers from Peter's throat but did not succeed. The fingers had become like stone around the throat of the dying man.

Peter's hand rose and touched Ierotheos wrist. In his eyes, a look of serenity and tacit acceptance arose; he had an honorable death. His life came to an end, but the man did what he had been trained for, from his Knight's battalion. He had the same death, thousands of other Knights had in the depths of ages. He was protecting humanity. He was giving his life away, for the common good.

Father Ierotheos, whispering a prayer, moved away from Peter's dead body and returned to his original position. The sounds from the gap were now very close. The monsters were coming. The priest stood firmly and got ready. Suddenly, the room was illuminated by the light of powerful headlamps. Petros and the other knights had arrived. The victory in this first battle was in favor of humanity.

As for the other battles that led to the war against the monsters, raging nowadays, as well as the mistakes that have been made, I will describe them to you my friend another time. If I describe them to you in a school hall, it will be History. If I describe them to you while we are somewhere hidden, it will be an update for you to join the fight. If I describe them to you after many years in front of a fireplace, then my friend, it will surely be an Adult FairyTale.

Short Story 3: The Chest

The cold, made his bones grind. He was forced to hold his hood with his hand, because the air was too strong. In front of him, he could see the towering walls of the city. It would be truly impossible to get in, without some help. He whistled once more as hard as he could, because the strength of the air almost nullified every sound. Time was passing and there was no movement. It would be a shame, his journey to be in vain. All that time on the road. All that effort and trouble. A life's dream, at the edge of completion.

At first, he thought he was wrong, but then, slowly, the dim light he had distinguished for a single moment, took the form of a torch. A small iron door had been opened, just enough to fit the hand that held the torch. His unknown partner had finally come. At last, he could pass to the last part of his journey.

He lowered his hood, low over his face and slowly walked to the door. Above the walls, he could hear the guards whisper. He stepped forward and the small door closed behind him. He was finally inside the city's walls. He was following the steps on which, four of his ancestors had walked before him.

He felt a clumsy touch on his back. He pulled out of his cloak a small sachet with gold and gave it to the man standing behind him. The man gave him the torch and with the same hand grabbed the sachet. He took a fleeting look of his face as the man was turning around, disappearing into darkness.

All he managed to see were two empty eyes. He took out the map. The map his father had made for him, before getting lost into the quest that now depended on himself. He had done the same thing for his own son, and for four hundred years, all the fathers of his family for their sons.

He took a last look at the map gently fondling it with his finger and started walking. He did not have a long distance to cover, but no one should realize his existence. He had to walk through the city like a shadow and reach the temple.

Coming out of the walls and entering the city, he saw with pleasure that the lighting was dim. Just a torch every one to two hundred meters allowing one to barely see his way to walk. He flung the torch in the corridor that passed under the walls and closed the wooden door. He stood still for a moment to get his eyes accustomed to the half-light and then, entered the city.

He could see the temple in the center of the city, protruding over the low houses, like the backbone of a monster preparing to devour them. From somewhere around him, he heard voices. There were people talking loudly, not worrying if someone could listen to them.

"For sure, one of the city lord's patrols", he thought.

Just a few feet away, he saw a stack of wood and next to it, the cart with which they had carried them up there. Walking low from one wall to the other, he hid beneath the cart. A few minutes later, the patrol passed in front of him and stopped after a few feet. He heard their voices once more.

"Hell" he thought, "Couldn't they stop somewhere else?"

Seconds were passing like hours. Had he delayed more, he would not have finished before the first light of dawn. The priests would enter the temple, they would find him and all his journey would be futile.

At last, the patrol continued its course. He came out of his hiding place and continued walking toward the temple. He could see the enormous - carved with images of hell - door. There was no lock on the temple's door. The images that decorated the door were like a thousand padlocks for the villagers of this city. The nobles simply did not care to go in.

Running with caution, he crossed the road. He opened the door a niche and walked in. A smile found its way to his face. He was close, he was very close. All he had to do was to find the blind wall behind the statue and go down to the basement. He looked around. In every corner of the aisle, there was a statue; one statue for every High Priest of the Temple. He had to find the statue of Sextus, the first High Priest of the temple.

In a distance, to the left of the sanctuary, he saw him. He could never forget his ugly face. He had been seeing it every day of his life as a child in his father's book. He had been seeing it almost every night in his dreams. It was he who dishonored his ancestor. He was the one who had destroyed the name of his family.

With decisive steps, he passed behind the statue. The void was there. The entrance to the basement was in common view, but no one could see it in the darkness that covered the back of the huge statue. He rode down the stairs leading to the basement. His journey was coming to completion. In front of him, just a few meters from his touch, was the chest that would bring light to the darkness that drowned his family for four hundred years.

He looked at the chest and felt his feet trembling. It took him almost a lifetime to find it. Now, he had it in front of his eyes and he could not believe it. It was exactly as he had imagined. Made of red wood and covered with white leather. At the point where the lid was touching the bottom part, it had a thin line of silver or something similar. It could also be made of ivory. The lock holding the chest's cover was sculptured by hand. The design that decorated it, though beautifully crafted, did not make any clear sense.

He took a deep breath, trying to calm down. The moment he waited for so many years; the legacy of his family, the end of a search that began four hundred years ago at a monastery in Constantinople. All would over today.

Four members of his family had already been lost in this quest during these four centuries. The end of time was now and the completion would be given by him.

Pride flooded his heart. Now, the souls of his ancestors could continue their journey. They would meet the supreme creator and sit on his right. The name of his family would once again acquire its old glory.

With tears in his eyes, he knelt and looked at the lock closely. It was nothing special. He would be able to open it easily. His mind went to Constantius, the family's head; a man who honored both his generation and God. The same man stigmatized by dishonesty, when he was accused of having drafted with the demon. The conquerors of Constantinople, being unable to get rid of him in any other way, tarnished his name. They destroyed him, with false and unfair categories. They caused him to disappear from the face of the Earth. Today, all this would end.

He pulled out if his cloak's inner pocket, the tools that would help him unlock the chest. The tools that would allow him to bring to light the evidence that everything said so many centuries ago were lies. He took two thin wires in his hands, turned and bent at the appropriate points, and approached his face near the carved lock. Its design began to make sense by looking at it from such a close distance. It represented a hunched man with his scary mouth open. His tongue, wide and wavy, looked in a vulgar way toward a line of men in cloaks. The men were four and stood in line, one after the other.

He cleansed his mind and checked his breath. With fixed fingers, he placed the wires in the lock. With gentle movements, he spotted the contact points of the mechanism and a few seconds later, he heard the coveted sound of unlocking. He let the wires fall from his hands and stood up. He caught the lid and, with a sharp decisive move, opened it.

At first, he did not see anything at all. A strange darkness covered the inside of the chest. It looked as though, for some reason, the light could not get inside it. A moment later, he saw a red glow coming from somewhere deep inside, toward him. The chest could not be so deep. What his eyes were saying to him, was absurd.

The glow continued to approach him with increasing speed. The man took a step back; one step, which however, did not bring any profit. The glow covered the space around him and filled his eyes, his soul and mind.

The chest closed by itself. The man had disappeared. In the carving of the lock, there were now five men in cloaks in front of the demon. The chest had been fed for another century.

Short Story 4: The Old Man and the Forest

The forest looks dark like the night sky from where the old man is sitting. The trees grow close to each other, reminding of lovers in an endless embracement. The light is passing softly through the foliage crowning the huge trunks, falling and disappearing into the dense low vegetation of the soil. The old man can really understand why his uneducated and faithful to prejudices grandmother, was telling him - when he was a little boy - to stay away from this particular part of his village.

He still remembers, in his late nineties today, and after all the years he spent in the psychiatric clinic, his grandmother talking about fairies and elves, for fellow villagers who had entered the forest and never returned. As a child, of course, he was afraid and never crossed the boundaries made by the huge trunks. Later, by the time he reached puberty, before he became ill, he began to believe that the forest was a dangerous place for young children and that, this was the reason his grandmother was telling him no to go there. He still avoids the forest. There are some things, which grow roots in your mind and never leave.

He can still remember the case of a young boy who was lost for two nights with his girlfriend in the dense forest. The girl was never found and the lad ended mentally ill. They had found him wandering alone in a miserable state, far away from the last houses of the village. The locals were talking back then about pregnancy and murder.

While the old man lives through his scattered memories, a few feet beyond the place where his eyes fall, two young kids walk hand by hand on a path that goes straight into the forest. It has already begun to darken, and their excitement, beyond the fact that they are alone away from indiscreet looks, is also increased by the light fear they feel. The boy, Paul, is of course not frightened or better, that is what he says.

"Come on, Sasha. I am with you, what are you afraid of? Would I ever allow anyone to harm you?"

The girl, Sasha, smiles. On one hand, she is afraid, but on the other, the more the boy talks to her, the more beautifully she feels. She is in love with him since primary school. The girl feels today that her craziest dream becomes reality.

Paul looks like an ancient god to her eyes. The boy is handsome; his beautiful eyes stand almost two heads above hers and his long shiny hair move lightly from the light breeze. There were a lot of times she had wondered what it was about her that he likes, but since he does, Sasha doesn't care. She will allow him today, to give her their first kiss.

All the villagers are weird. Even when they just walk together after school, they can hear them whisper. The kids are a couple for almost a month now, but because of the school and the village, they have only managed to hold each other's hand. The village is small and the people curious. They are already sixteen and they must not give them any reason to talk about.

Their luck changed the morning their teacher made them a team for a biology project. They had to go to the forest and find various insects and plants. Sasha didn't even care if she wanted to touch them. She had an excuse to disappear with Paul in the woods, under the blessings of the school.

"Sasha, why don't we sit for a while?" Paul's voice sounds just before he gently wraps his arms around her.

He loves that girl; she is so small that looks like a doll in his hands. He rests gently on a fallen tree and looks deep into her eyes. Their lips touch and the golden wings of magic make their young hearts tremble. Time seems to have stopped, no sound is heard. The world includes just the two of them. Paul gently touches her face.

"I hope this moment will never end" he whispers.

He sees tears flowing from her black eyes and with the thumb of his right hand, wipes them off.

"These are tears of happiness" Sasha says. "I've been waiting for this kiss for a long time."

Paul turns his head to the side, as looking at something. He does not want the girl to see the dampness of his own eyes. Men do not cry. What he sees, however, surprises him. A few centimeters from his face, stands a bug. It really stands there, immovable at the same place. It does not dangle its wings and it does not fly. It just stands at the same spot, as if hanging from invisible threads.

"Sasha, look!" he says, turning his face toward the girl.

The girl's eyes are fixed to a point just above him and her lips tremble.

"Paul, what is happening? I can't hear anything but us. Something feels wrong".

The lad takes her hand and pulls her softly toward him.

"Let's go! I do not like it here. "

The trees become thicker as the kids are walking. Their leaves almost hide the sun. Then, they see him. Paul tightens the girl's hand and pulls her behind him. In the middle of the path, a man stands. He only wears an old, really worn out pair of trousers. His body is dark and shines like ebony. His bare feet are muddy as if he walks in the forest permanently without ever wearing shoes.

"Good evening" says the boy.

The man just stays motionless. He does not seem to hear or even perceive the presence of the kids.

"Good evening" Paul says again.

The man's face finally moves. He raises his eyes to the height of Paul's face and looks at him. The man's face is sprightly, he seems to be thinking. His gaze begins to travel over Paul's face until he notices Sasha that can barely be seen behind him.

With a slow movement of his head, the branches of the trees begin to sift and move. The two kids look around, unable to believe what they see. The branches are lowering more and as if they were hands, lock the boy in between them and lift him high above the ground.

Paul hears a terrible sound but almost immediately, realizes that he hears his own voice. He is screaming like a baby. He tries to bring himself together; to expel the fear that overwhelms his soul. At the back of his mind, he knows that he has to find a way to react. He has to take out of this situation himself and above all, Sasha. The man still looks at him with his empty dark eyes.

His gaze falls on Sasha and begins to travel smuttily over her youthful body.

"You are beautiful" he says. "You will give me good sons."

Sasha unconsciously takes a step back, but hits on wood. The trees that have grabbed Paul have encircled them. There is no way out.

The man's eyes travel again at Paul.

"Do you mind if I make her mine?"

A grumpy chuckle, a ruddy laugh, sounds from somewhere within him and the tip of his tongue comes a little out of his mouth, like tasting the air.

Paul fights to escape from the trees that keep him tied, while blood is starting to flow from his hands and back. The branches are starting to penetrate his flesh.

"I prefer to die" he replies.

"I might fulfill your wish!" answers the man with a husky voice.

The man turns his gaze to Sasha and his lips whisper something indefinable. In a second, the face of the girl changes; her gaze loses its innocence. Girlishness disappears from her appearance and the girl now looks like a mature woman. Her eyes become deeper, more obscene. Paul turns his face away. This woman is not Sasha. She cannot be her.

Sasha's body rises. Her breasts are starting to look bigger. The woman, who looks like Sasha, the woman who normally Sasha would become after several years, caresses her hair and looks deep in the man's eyes.

"I want you" she whispers and walks toward him.

She gets in front of him and wraps her hands around him. The man smiles, looks at Paul for one last time and takes her up in his arms. Then, they both disappear among the trees.

***

"Newspaper: Kirikas of Evia
25 May 2005
Tragedy in a village of Evia!

On the 15th of the month, according to residents' testimonies, two students entered the forest for a school project. Both students disappeared, and although their fellow villagers and a large number of police officers searched, combing the forest, no trace of them was found. The locals said that since the boy and the girl where a couple, there was a possibility of pregnancy that might led them to live their houses, avoiding to face their parents.

Three days later, however, the body of the young man was found in the forest badly hurt. His wounds seemed to have been caused by animals, but the forensic scientist stated that the deadly blow had been given by a wooden object that penetrated his heart.

Police investigations continue..."

***

The old man is sitting in the courtyard of his home, touching the newspaper on a small table next to his coffee. He looks at the forest. For some reason, the treatment that began many years ago in the psychiatric clinic, does not allow him to understand what the newspaper article reminds him of. He can only remember the face of his late grandmother. A single tear flows from his dull eyes. Who knows? Maybe the tear is for his grandmother, perhaps for the kids the newspaper is talking about, or for a young boy, who many years ago saw something that he shouldn't, lost a loved one and ended up in a hospital for the mentally ill...

Short Story 5: The Call

He loved the sea throughout his entire life. He was always feeling, since his childhood, that the sea was calling him. Nevertheless, he never found the ideal job or place to be, to feel close enough. There was always something wrong. He worked in the sea for a number of years. He became a sailor since a really young age. When he realized that it was not what he really wanted, the thing that would complete his life, he bought a tavern by the sea. That wasn't what he wanted either. Although he was practically always there, working, sleeping, living with her sounds, smelling the salty taste of the sea, something was always missing.

He was almost forty years old when the dreams began. Every night, he was seeing a particular beach. He could see the silver moon leaning against the water, coming almost straight to his feet. The rocks mirrored in the dark water, like a painting with dark, deep colors. Next to the water, there was in his dream a small handcrafted pier. It was made just out of ten boards and had a small wooden boat, tied on it, dancing by the light breeze. Somewhere around him, in his dream, he could hear a female voice calling him.

He realized that if he wanted to finally follow this call, he would have to find the beach; his beach. He would have to find out, to whom the voice belonged. He left the tavern, sold his belongings and bought a motorcycle. The beach in his dream seamed Mediterranean. He couldn't be wrong because he was born just outside the city of Sangre, in Portugal. On the one side of his small village, were the Mediterranean coasts and on the other, the Atlantic coasts. He could easily understand their differences, no matter how small they were.

He picked up the few things he needed for the trip, loaded the bike and left. His plan was to follow the Mediterranean coasts, starting from his city and going all the way to Tangier, in Morocco. If his beach weren't there, he would start wandering around the countless islands.

The trip was long and every beach more beautiful than the others. Some were filled with tourists and others, deserted and difficult to approach. Time went by; his mind was overwhelmed by beauty. His love for the sea continued to fill his life. The call, however, was not completed.

Several months later, he reached the beautiful Algiers. The beach was naturally wonderful like all the others he had seen, people were friendly and the water calm, but once more, the beach of his dreams wasn't there. The beach, from where the woman's voice was calling him, was nowhere to be seen. He has started getting tired. He had left his little tavern in the middle of winter, another winter had pass by, the summer had come and still, nothing.

He stopped his bike next to a small café. He ordered something cool to drink and took in his hands a magazine that was left on the table. He wanted to use it more as a fan, to cool his red from the sun face, rather than read it. After all, he could not even read the language. He began to dangle it, enjoying the dew, when he froze. There, on the front page, was the beach. Something was written in the wavy letters they used in Algeria and right below, was a photo of the small pier and the boat. He felt his eyes wet and a longing in his soul. He had found the beach. He had finally found his beach.

He called the waiter and showed him the magazine. He tried with his little French to find where the photo had been taken. The waiter was initially confused, but suddenly a glow appeared in his eyes.

"Carte" he told him, "map", and showed him the backpack he had placed on the motorcycle's tank.

In the outer pocket was the map of the area he had with him. He stood up and gave the map to the waiter. He placed it on the table and pulled a pencil from his pocket; he drew a path on the map and looked up, smiling at him.

"Muito obrigado" were the only words his lips could form.

He threw a bill on the table, grabbed the map and the magazine, raced to the motorcycle and left for the last part of his journey and the call of his entire life.

Before the dawn of the next day, he had reached his beach. Everything was exactly the same with the picture he was seeing every night in his dreams. He could see the two mountains on both sides of the inlet, lowering and touching the water; the blond, fine sand that hugged and wormed his bare feet. He could see right in front of him, the small wooden pier, entering the water for just a few meters. Even the boat was there, tied with a rope on one of the small pier's feet.

His heart was ready to explode. Although he had not found the woman yet, he felt he was closer than ever to his destination. Walking through the sand and taking off his t-shirt, he dove into the sea. The warm water immediately eradicated the fatigue from his body. He let himself free and felt the water lifting his body.

He closed his eyes and shouted, without caring if anyone would hear him.

"Estou aqui, cheguei", I'm here, I have come.

An hour later, he stepped out of the water and lay down on the beach. His heart filled with peace. All he still had to do was to find the woman calling him in his dreams. He believed or rather knew that it was just a matter of time. In his dream, her voice sounded when the moon was high above the sea. He would wait. He would wait for her, no matter how long it would take him.

He took his backpack from his bike and pulled out the map and the magazine. He placed them in front of him on the sand and stayed there, staring at them for hours. When he raised his head again and stared at the horizon, the moon was in the right position. The image that he saw was that of his dreams.

He stood up and walked to the wooden pier. From somewhere away, he heard a woman's voice calling him. He walked faster and climbed on the pier. At its end, he saw a hand with long beautiful fingers touching the wood and then, the smiling face of a beautiful young woman emerging. The water flowed over her soft features, giving her the silver tint of the moon. Her dark, long hair was falling wet on her white shoulders, almost covering her firm bosom.

Enchanted by her beauty, he smiled back. The woman's right hand got up and gave him a soft nod, inviting him to approach her. The emptiness he had, since his childhood in the depths of his soul, had now been filled. The few steps left to reach the woman, would lead him to completion.

Sun had taken the place of the moon and the silver color of the night had given way to the golden brightness of the day. A dark haired man approached the motorcycle slowly. He saw a t-shirt thrown in the sand and next to it, a backpack, a map and a magazine. He looked around and saw no one. His gaze embraced the silver water, and then, crouching, he took the magazine in his hands. He pulled his Djellaba a little higher and sat quietly on the sand.

Flipping through the magazine, he saw in a photograph the very beach he was now standing on. The article was about a tale of a sea monster, whose upper body was that of a beautiful young woman and the rest was that of a huge snake. The legend was that she was looking for the descendants of all sailors who had escaped wreckages at the time of the colonies, calling them and taking them to the place their ancestors had escaped from. When a place for someone in the dark depths of the sea opens, according to the myth, it would be covered, even after a thousand years.

Short Story 6: Teddy Bears

We moved with my wife to the suburbs about a year ago. We, like many of the people who live in the big cities, were looking for the peace and quiet, the suburbs offer so generously. My daily journey to go and come back from my office was now a way for me to relax. I really loved the large, almost always empty, avenue, which was adorned on both sides with trees and greenery. I even started drinking my morning coffee on the way and in the afternoon when I was coming back, thanks to this route, I was forgetting everything about work and I was going home calm and without any worries.

Earlier this month, however, something changed. At a certain point on the route, I started to feel uncomfortable. I had the strange feeling that someone was looking at me. Whenever I passed by that same place, I was looking around me to find the cause of this strange feeling. I began to feel angry, because that was the road I was taking every day to go and come back from work. I started avoiding this road as much as possible; making an excessively big circle that was spoiling my calm, but also making me go late to work.

Yesterday, I took the decision to go over there and try to find out why I felt that way. I found the reason the moment I opened my car's door. For some strange reason, the owner of a store had hanged high on his fence, three stuffed teddy bears; not the teddy bears we buy for children but the huge ones we usually give to our Valentine girl.

During the time they were hung, the rain and the dirt from the road had made the teddy bears disgusting. The one to the right, had one of its eyes taken off and its head was unnaturally hung sideways. They were in general, in a miserable condition and for some strange reason they were scaring my head off. I was too afraid even to look at them.

I had to find a way to get them down, so I wouldn't have to look at them every day. I couldn't bear them. I could not understand why I was so afraid of them, since they were just dolls and nothing else. Nevertheless, it was impossible for me to see them hanging over my head, or rather feel them looking at me.

So I decided, instead of making anything stupid and take them down, because I would probably have to face the owner of the store, to deal with them. So, I decided to go there, late at night, and face them as a real man. I would stand in front of them and have a cigarette while looking into their eyes.

Wednesday was the big day. I came home from work, using a different road of course. I told my wife that I would go for a beer with some friends around ten o'clock, I ate and then I went to bed. I got up at nine and a little later I took off. I felt my palms sweaty on the steering wheel as I was driving and my feet shaking, but I was determined. I would go and I would cope with my fear. I am a forty-year-old man, I cannot be afraid of some stupid dirty teddy bears.

I arrived at the point and parked my car at the end of the road. I walked across and stood in front of the fence. I raised my head and saw them. They were hanging high over my head and their blind eyes were looking away at the mountain. Eventually, they were not nearly as scary as I thought. I relaxed a bit and lit a cigarette. I laughed at myself for my stupidity. How was it possible for a man like me to be so scared of these simple kids' toys? I looked up again smiling, only to figure out that the hanging bears were just two.

I felt my mouth dry and I looked around. Within seconds, all street lights went out and I could only see the lights of some houses far away. The silence was absolute and I saw no car approaching me. I tried to move in order to get to my car, but my feet seemed stuck on the sidewalk. No matter how hard I was trying, I could not make the slightest move. The lower part of my body was frozen. I could, however, move the rest.

I stretched my hand in the back pocket of my trouser and got my cell phone. I desperately needed some light. I brought it in front of me and turned on the phone's lens. I started to move around in a totally stupid way like a pendulum, as my legs were still stuck on the sidewalk. I heard the door of the store opening, producing a sound that reminded me strongly of scary movies on television. It was the same sound that when you hear, you begin to shout to the actor to get the hell away from wherever he is.

I bent my body to the side, to look through the door. The darkness was absolute and to be honest, only the thought of pointing the phone's light in there, terrified me more than the situation I was in. I heard the sound of a car behind me and turned my head. At last someone was coming; someone who could probably help me. What I saw surpassed even the craziest scenarios. My car was leaving. No one was sitting in the driver's seat, but the car was leaving.

I probably screamed, I'm not sure however, seeing my car leaving; something so intimate and mine abandoning me, every logical thought disappeared from within my head. I began to hit my legs with my hands to force them to move, and they did. Very slowly of course, and with movements that would be reasonable only in water, I started to walk and tried to move away from the fence.

As slow as my movements were, so quickly the fence's door opened. Teddy bears of all sizes and colors began to emerge from within. They all still had a common point. Their heads were real. Their eyes were red like the flames of Hell and were staring at me. But this time, they really were looking at me. Their mouths were wide-opened, and large, dark-colored teeth with a rough surface, covered with foam that rolled over them falling on the pavement, protruded from inside.

I was trying to run, to move a little faster and get away to save myself. I was screaming and crying, but I kept moving like I was sunk in something thick. All my body seemed to move in slow motion. The teddy bears were almost on me. A few seconds later, I felt the first bite on my leg. They were cutting pieces out of my legs. I could feel my flesh tearing apart and being consumed by the diabolical creatures that were hunting me.

The pain took hold of me. I fell to the ground and saw them rushing over me. Now, their rough teeth were dangling all over my body. I tried to cover my face with my hand, but before I could get it in front of my eyes, I felt teeth getting on my cheek, I felt my blood flowing in my throat, choking me. I could not even scream. The only sound I could make was a strange gurgling sound.

I closed my eyes and waited for the end. I felt my body being split and pulled to a thousand directions, at the same time. Beyond the mumbles, combined with the sound of my flesh being chewed, I heard something else; something similar to a voice. I tried to concentrate; to understand what the voice was saying. I could not do anything else. My end was close. It was a voice. It was a woman's voice. I tried to control myself and forget the pain, to understand what it was saying. I finally did.

The voice was clearly feminine and I could hear her say:

"Wake up love; you'll be late for your beer appointment with your friends! Oh come on, wake up."

I stood up, looking around. I felt my head hurt, like being locked in a vise. Everything was a dream; just a stupid nightmare, coming from my absurd fear for those kid's toys. My determination seemed to be lost, but I would insist on my decision. I would go to deal with them in reality.

I got dressed; I kissed my wife and stepped into my car. A few minutes later, I reached the store with the fence and parked my car at the edge of the road. I walked across and stood in front of the fence. I raised my head and saw them. They were hanging high over my head and their blind eyes were looking away on the mountain. I relaxed a bit and lit a cigarette. I laughed at myself for my stupidity. How was it possible for a man like me to be scarred by some simple teddy bears? I looked up again smiling and at the same time, I realized that I was living my dream for real. Only two teddy bears were hung on the fence and I was sure that this time, I would not hear a voice calling me to wake up...

Short Story 7: Romphaea

"Romphaea or Maellartach: One of the Mortal Instruments given to the Nephilim by the Angel Raziel. It is a large and beautiful sword, its most distinguishable feature being a guard that looks like a golden pair of wings. It is said to be the blade used to drive Adam and Eve from the Garden of Eden. It is also known as The Mortal Sword, the Soul Sword, and the Angel blade."

Peace and quiet were shrouding the desolate land. Although it was noon, thick clouds were preventing the sunshine from touching the earth. The world was dressed in shades of gray. The whole place seemed to be devoid of color.

Suddenly the clouds parted and golden fire flowed through the opening. The flames touched the gray land enveloping it in all the colors of the rainbow. And in the midst of it all, a resounding noise. The sound of trumpets announcing an arrival.

The spot where the flames touched the ground swelled, cracked and opened. Through it a human form emerged. The form stretched and pure white wings unfolded from its back, their greatness and beauty transforming the gray land into a fusion of brilliant colors.

***

The man opens his eyes. He gently lifts his head and stares at his limbs strapped on the bed. Wide leather straps tight around his wrists, his ankles and his waist. He's dressed in plain white cotton clothes. He hears a noise from his right and, with much effort, turns his head towards the source.

"Are you awake, Angel?" a woman's voice says.

He looks into her eyes and then his gaze slides towards the needle she sticks into the bulging veins of his arm.

"Time to get back to sleep", he hears the woman saying, right before he sinks back into oblivion.

***

A siren is wailing in the background as police cars are flooding the hospital's entrance. People are running outside through the doors, some of them wearing light blue overalls, some of them white. Those with the light blue ones are doctors, the rest of them nurses.

Let's head closer and listen. Don't be afraid, no one will see us. We'll be in and out like the wind. As we get closer a man with light blue overalls also approaches the policemen. His face shows fear and anxiety. Come, let's get even closer, he's saying something to them.

"The Angel escaped; we have no idea how long ago or how."

***

Heavy dark buildings covered in soot are blocking his view. They rise high above his head leaving only a gray and depressing sliver of sky exposed. He can't take it any longer. Ever since he arrived in this world he lives in torment. He was sent here to evaluate the course of mankind. To see if they deserve our Lord's grace.

Yes, the man's name is Sariel and he's an Angel of the Lord. He shed his angelic form and became one of us. He feels dirty. Our primitive smell burns his nostrils, our filthy touch disgusts him. We have received the most gifts of all the Lord's children. Even more than those granted to the ones belonging to His army.

We were given free will. We were given a beautiful, bright and verdant world. We were given the gift of love. We were given everything and all that was asked from us was to live in harmony with ourselves and with all the other glorious creations of our Lord.

We destroyed everything. We take each other's lives with pleasure and ascribe it to His will. We destroy the planet without any thought of the consequences. We torture animals; even those we keep close to us as pets because supposedly we love them.

He can't tolerate us any longer. We've done enough. His orders were to arrive, to inspect and to leave. That's not enough for him. Our corruption is so massive that we must get hurt. We must experience first-hand the consequences of our actions.

Heavy dark buildings covered in soot are cloaking his revenge in their shadows. They rise high above his head hiding him from the eyes of the Lord. He looks at the gray and depressing sliver of sky and realizes he is absolutely right. He realizes his actions are justified.

He has evaluated us. We are not worthy of the Lord's grace.

In front of him is another one of us. The man is lying on the street writhing in agony with Sariel's romphaea penetrating his vile mortal carcass. Blood, scarlet and filthy flows towards the Angel's feet. He pulls his romphaea with force and thrusts it into the body for a second time. More blood. Gushing and sticking on him, on his clothes and on his face. He feels the strong metallic taste on his lips.

The carcass is empty. The body is still. He hears voices all around him. Someone is screaming.

"They finally realize the burden of their sins", he's thinking. "They understand that my revenge is the only thing they deserve."

More of us approach him. Filthy humans. Parasites on the back of the wonderful world our Lord has given them. They wear blue uniforms and have their guns raised. Someone strikes him on his back. The romphaea falls from his hand and he falls on the street right next to it. He closes his eyes so he won't have to see their faces. He despises them.

Someone is tying his hands behind his back. People keep screaming all around him.

"Despicable, foolish creatures. Unworthy abusers of the gifts that were given to you."

He opens his eyes. On the street, where his sword had fallen, a long knife now sways. They turn his face towards the sky. He stares at the man holding his chin straight in the eyes.

"I am not afraid of you", the Angel says. "You're the ones who should be afraid of me. I am the Lord's vengeance!"

***

The man opens his eyes. He gently lifts his head and stares at his limbs strapped on the electric chair. Wide leather straps tight around his wrists, his ankles and his waist. He's dressed in plain white cotton clothes. On his right a priest is standing. He hears a voice.

"You have been sentenced to death and today you will be punished for your crimes. This is your last chance to repent in the eyes of the Lord."

The man keeps laughing as they put a wet cloth in his mouth and cover his head with a hood. His voice is muffled but clear:

"I will come back soon to finish what I started."

***

Peace and quiet are shrouding the desolate land. Although it is noon, thick clouds are preventing the sunshine from touching the earth. The world is dressed in shades of gray. The whole place seems to be devoid of color.

Suddenly the clouds part and golden fire flows through the opening. The flames touch the gray land enveloping it in all the colors of the rainbow. And in the midst of it all a resounding noise. The sound of trumpets announcing an arrival.

The spot where the flames touch the ground swells, cracks and opens. Through it a human form emerges. The form stretches and pure white wings unfold from its back, their greatness and beauty transforming the gray land into a fusion of brilliant colors...

Short Story 8: Darkness

Darkness in the soul can take many forms. It may enter the soul suddenly after an event or be transferred there in the form of a virus by someone who carries it within. There are, however, occasions like Elijah's, when darkness nests in the soul, accompanies it in all its travels, in all its stances and in all the lives one will be sent to live on this Earth. This darkness can be defeated only by the redemptive power of fire.

Elijah externally seemed like a wonderful man, measured and serious. He was a technical high school teacher, and both his friends and his students loved him. The darkness in his soul, however, was always there, well hidden from sight, covering an important part of his thoughts.

As long as Elijah was a child, when darkness was awaking in him, he directed it on the defenseless pets of the neighborhood, in which he and his family were living. His father was an army officer and their family was moving frequently. This did not allow Elijah to be connected to the dead and dismembered pets left behind after they were gone.

When Elijah grew up and got a place of his own, he understood the danger his neighbors represented and tried to find other ways to calm the darkness in his soul. The vast world of the internet gave him the way out he was looking for. He discovered many websites where amateur writers specializing in murder and blood stories shared the darkness of their morbid fantasies and asked for the opinions and comments of the others.

Writing down all the things he wanted to do and did not dare, he won the respect and acceptance of the other writers, while at the same time he managed to keep the dark beast inside him, asleep.

One day, one of his internet friends sent him a message, stating that all his stories were repeating the same pattern, and that if he ever wanted to become a real writer, he would have to gain some experience. A good writer, he continued, puts himself in his hero's place and thinks like his hero would think.

"Only if you become your hero, you will be able to determine his course and behavior. If you do not become your hero, your stories will never be truthful enough".

Elijah received the comment very negatively. Who on earth did he thought he was. How would he even dare talking to him like that, telling him that his stories were not believable enough? After all, his hands were painted with real blood; blood of animals, but still. He had seen souls leaving bodies by his own hands; he had felt bones crushing by his own blows...

The darkness inside him started breathing again, demanded vengeance and Elijah to start hunting again. This time, however, he would not be hunting animals. This stage had been surpassed many years ago. Animals were not enough for him anymore. He would go hunting people and the stories he would write would be real.

He kept his decision within and let it flood his soul. When he felt ready, full and strong, he went out for his first hunt. His hero would be a hunter, a hunter who sweeps injustice and becomes judge and executor at the same time. His name... Bellerophontes. Like the ancient Greek hero and warrior who killed Chimera.

His first hunt took place on a Saturday night. He took the weapon of his dead father, filled it up and climbed to the hill of Philopappou. He began to walk looking for an excuse; any reason for justice, or rather, that was what he was thinking in order to forget the dangers of the act he intended to do. No one would condemn a hero, someone who acts against injustice.

In the forest, under the monument, he heard voices. Some guy was fighting with a girl. Bellerophontes, approached them silently, hidden behind the trees. The darkness within him overwhelmed his existence. Only by being there, the adrenaline flooding his body, was giving him a hero's strength.

He saw them. The girls' hand was locked inside the man's fingers and he was yelling at her with a sharp voice. She was crying. She was in pain, trying to escape from him. Bellerophontes came closer, lifted his jacket's hood and shouted to the man. He wanted to let him know he was there; he wanted to see the acceptance of the end in his eyes. The man looked straight at him, with no fear at all, and asked him what he wanted. The weapon came up almost by its own will and pointed straight to the man's head.

The girl screamed and freed herself, but stood still, looking at Bellerophontes. Fear was filing her existence and brought a smile to the hero's face. The gun poured metal and smoke into the man's face. Blood and bone fragments blew on the hands and face of Bellerophontes. The girl fainted. Without even giving her one look, he started walking back to his car. Darkness was fed and new stories were ready to be written.

The next day, Elijah uploaded the story to the site. The description of the murder scene was complete and illustrative and the comments were enthusiastic. Elijah asked the guy who had criticize him for his opinion. His message came after a while. It was good, he wrote, but the gun did all the work, the hero just pulled the trigger. There was no sense of the killing in the hands of the murderer, there was no direct contact.

Elijah's eyes opened widely, he felt his hurt beating in his brain. He felt like, all the blood of his body was gathered in his head, trying to find a way out. The stranger kept playing with him, he continued challenging him. Elijah took a deep breath. His hurt started to beat slower.

"Ok", he thought. "Let's play your game. You want more? I will give you more".

He waited all week for darkness to overwhelm his soul. He kept his mind focused on his critic. He became Bellerophontes and kept his thought on his next murder. Everything would have to be perfect. As the week approached its end, Bellerophontes became the master of his body and soul. The hero re-emerged and became the guide of Elijah's thoughts and feelings.

It was finally Sunday. It was his day. Elijah wore the same dark colored clothes he used for his first murder. They still had the smell and the marks of his first victim's blood. For him, time was continuing from the moment he walked away, leaving the girl unconscious, next to her companion's dead body on the hill of Philopappou.

Elijah walked into his car and left. This time he was going to hunt next to the sea. The black color of the night sky, reflected on the water was a perfect match for the darkness in his soul. He had the perfect place in his mind. When he reached Kavouri, he turned right and began to descend to the beach. At the end of the road, he parked his car and stepped out. There were a lot of houses around him, but just as he remembered, there was a line of trees beside the sea, keeping the light from the houses away. The place was perfect, the time was perfect. He was perfect; he was a hero again.

Time was passing by and he couldn't hear a thing. He needed his next victim to do something bad; he had to have an excuse to calm his mind. Far, beyond the trees, the entrance light of a house turned on. A woman came out with a dog, talking on her cell phone. Bellerophontes felt that his time was approaching.

Walking slowly, he approached as closely as possible to hear what the woman was saying. His acts had to be justified. He was a hero-avenger and not a simple common assassin. The woman laughed and arranged an appointment with someone after her husband left for work. Adultery justified his actions, giving him the push he needed.

He took out his own phone and put it next to his ear. He came to the light and started approaching the woman. She saw him almost immediately, but did not feel threatened. She was accustomed of seeing people walking by the beach, talking on their phone or doing whatever they wanted to do, even late at night. She kept talking on her phone, laughing.

As soon as Bellerophontes came close enough, he rushed over her, closing her mouth with his hand. He gave her a strong punch in the stomach, forcing her to kneel. She dropped her phone and looked at him. Her eyes were wide open. Fear was now present, giving him exactly what he wanted.

The woman started begging him for her life. She told him that she had money inside the house; she would give him whatever he wanted. Her fear was feeding the darkness in his soul. She was now an easy prey for Elijah's hero. His next hit left her lying in his hands. He took her to the place he was hidden earlier and waited for her to wake up. He wanted her be looking into his eyes, the moment her soul would leave her body. He wanted to remember her last look; he had to describe it in his next story.

The woman opened her eyes. Her gaze was cloudy and disoriented. Before she could make the slightest sound, Bellerophontes' hands grasped her throat. Two of his thumbs began to push her trachea with increasing power. The air ceased to reach her lungs. Her face began to turn blue and her body started shaking. Her eyes seemed ready to be thrown out of their niches.

Bellerophontes took in every second of her last moments. The darkness within him was curling and spreading like a snake out of pleasure. The woman's body stopped moving. Her eyes were like mirrors, the image of his face, was clearly what she would take with her in her grave. Then, they froze into the nothingness of death.

Elijah's hero left her body on the ground and, with gentle moves, closed her eyes.

"Where you are going, there is nothing to see!" he whispered.

He stood up and looked down at his new victim lying in front of his feet. She looked like she was in the right place; low, down on earth.

He stared at his hands, still shaking from the force applied to her throat, but also from the pleasure he felt. He smiled and wearing his hood, got to his car, sat in the driver's seat and left. He had a new story to write.

First thing in the morning, the story was ready and uploaded. Congratulations in the comments were coming like rain. Everyone had something good to say, even to thank him for the journey to the imagination he offered them. Elijah, however, had eyes for one and only person. He was waiting for his critic's comment. He sat over his computer, waiting for his name to appear.

At exactly twelve o'clock, the stranger left his comment. He congratulated him for the creation of his hero and the way he described his feelings. Reading his comment, Elijah felt justified. The second part of the comment, however, angered him. The stranger told him that as far as the victim's feelings were concerned, he made not even the slightest mention. It was as if the woman was not a victim, but just a doll that got badly treated.

How on earth could he experience the feelings of a victim? How could he get into the victim's position and survive to describe it? For the first time, he decided to respond to the stranger's comment and ask him. Seconds later, he received a private message.

"I can help you if you want me to."

Elijah smiled; he had just found his next victim. The man's comments were written out of malice and nothing else. He was getting pleasure by being negative. Bellerophontes within Elijah was ready to take over once more.

"Very good", he replied. "I will accept your offer. Tell me, where and how we will do it!"

The man's message arrived almost immediately.

"Friday at midnight, in the old hotel in Parnitha. Come, park somewhere and leave the rest on me".

Elijah smiled, he had three days to prepare. He had three days to let the dark fill him and the expectation to become need. In three days, he would once again release Bellerophontes.

Friday came and Elijah was burning out of desire. The soul of the stranger was his. He had everything planned in his mind. He would shoot him but not kill him and then pull him into the abandoned building. He would only then kill him, slowly and agonizingly. He would enjoy every moment and as soon as the soul of his critic was gone, he would stop being Bellerophontes once and for all.

The road to the hotel was beautiful. It had a lot of turns, but the cool night breeze and the view below the mountain, gave Bellerophontes the time to calm down and draw the darkness inside. He thought over his plan once again and felt ready.

The lights of a car approaching him from behind at high speed, took him out of his dream. In front of him, there was a big turn and below it, a vast cliff. He pulled his car to the side and turned on the alarm lights to let the other car pass. The car stopped next to his open window.

"Good evening, my friend!" said the man behind the wheel and threw in his car something that looked like a bottle in flames.

He stood parked right next to him, until the fire spread inside the car and on Elijah's clothes. Then, he drove his car far ahead, allowing Elijah to open the door and get off.

Elijah could feel the liquid floating over his feet, wetting his trousers, followed by the fire. The pain was unbearable. Elijah screamed, his open mouth was trying at the same time to take a breath of fresh air, but the flames, the smoke and the sweet smell of his own body burning, wouldn't let him.

The heat of the fire was now touching his face. He felt his lips melting and his eyes dull. The pain had distanced him. It was like living the pain from afar, as if his body was not on fire. The last thing his eyes saw, before they were lost in the flames, was the man's face. His eyes showed that he loved every second of his torture. He was recording every moment and every scream of Elijah.

Elijah ceased to exist, once and for all. The darkness in his soul would never endanger earth again. He had been consumed by the redemptive power of fire. He had been annihilated.

A few days later, on the first page of a well-known newspaper, it was reported that a burned-out car was found, and next to it, the charred body of a man. On the pages of the same newspaper's cultural news, a special reference was made to the last book of a writer of mystery stories entitled "Death in flames". But no one made the slightest link between the two articles...

Short Story 9: Temporal Paradox

Wednesday, June 14 1999

The ship was about to reach the port of Piraeus when the first voices were heard. We were seated, me and my daughter, on the last deck, picking up our coffees and some oranges from the table, as the loudspeakers had just made the last announcement to the passengers that we were going to enter the port. We were returning from our first holiday together. I was divorced for many years and this was the first time her mother agreed to let us go on a trip together, for her fourteenth birthday.

The first voice that came to our ears was female.

"Stop, someone has fallen into the sea! Help!"

That voice was followed by others, and seconds later, everyone on the deck was running to the rails of the ship to see what was happening. About 10 meters away from the ship, there was a man in the sea, yelling in our direction. His face seemed very familiar to me, but I could not associate it with a name.

While I was wondering why his face looked so familiar, a siren sounded and the ship began to cut speed and turn towards him. The crew of the ship threw life jackets in the water and as soon as we reached him, the catapult of the ship opened and two men dug into the sea. A few minutes later, we saw the crew pulling the man up the catapult and covering him with a jacket.

At that very moment, panic erupted. There was a huge explosion, and the ship tilted with its metal creaking from the pressure it received. The blast wave of the explosion threw both me and my daughter on the rails and we felt the bodies of the people behind, hitting on us. The explosion was followed by a wave in the sea, which gave the ship another hard hit. I felt that if I laid my hand, I could touch the water.

The ship began to lean to its side, throwing us all on the floor. I embraced my daughter who looked at me with her eyes huge from horror. We were still alive. Around us, as the ship tried to return to its original position, we heard people weeping and crying of pain and despair. I could see several bodies lying permanently on the floor; people who had made the last trip of their lives.

The ship managed to reach the port with the help of the coastguard and we were loaded on ambulances and taken to the hospital. Fortunately, both my daughter and I had nothing more than bruises and scratches. I had two broken ribs, but my daughter was fine.

The news said that more than fifty people had died and that at least twice as many were hospitalized in a critical situation. It was also said, that the explosion had been caused by a mechanism on the left side of the ship. The same side me and my daughter were sitting. If we haven't gone to see the man in the sea, we would both have been dead. In the count of the ship's passengers, according to the TV always, only people with tickets and the crew members were found. The man; our savior, was never found. He must have fallen back into the sea and drowned, there was no other explanation...

Wednesday, June 14 1999

The ship was about to reach the port of Piraeus when the first voices were heard. At a table on the last deck, a man and a girl were seated. They were picking up their coffees and some oranges from the table because the loudspeakers had just made the final announcement for the passengers, to get ready to disembark.

There was a huge explosion, and the ship tilted with its metal creaking from the pressure it received. The blast wave of the explosion, totally destroyed the side of the ship were the man and the girl were seated. The explosion was followed by a wave in the sea, which gave the ship another hard hit, forcing it to almost touch the water.

A few seconds later, the ship began to lean towards its other side, throwing all the passengers on the floor. As the ship struggled to return to its original position, one could hear people crying and screaming of pain and despair. The deck was covered with bodies lying permanently on the floor; people who had made the last trip of their lives. Among them was a man, covered in blood, screaming desperately, embracing a dead fourteen-year-old girl.

The ship finally managed to reach the port with the help of the coastguard and ambulances took the wounded people and transferred them to the hospital. The news said that more than fifty people had died and that at least twice as many people were hospitalized in a critical condition. According to the TV always, the explosion was caused by a mechanism on the left side of the ship.

Wednesday, June 14 2015

I finally managed, three months ago, to find a way to get back to the past. I will finally be able to save my girl. All these years, I never ceased to wonder why she should be dead and not me. Why did God allowed the soul of an innocent girl to be lost, before she could even see the beauties of life? She had never harmed anyone. All she did was to give joy to the life of people around her with her smile. Children must not leave before their parents. It's horrible. It is absurd and destroys the very essence of the world.

During the first years, I wanted to kill myself; to leave, and join her high in the sky. I begged God to keep me and send her back to earth. I was willing to go wherever He wanted me to go; it would be the same for me, as long as she was alive. Her mother called me a killer. She said that it was my fault, she was lost.

"I know it", I replied and with my eyes not even daring to cry, I left her home and never saw her again.

Five years ago, a scientist stated on television that in a while, time travels would be a reality. This man was Greek and worked in a big organization in Switzerland. I left everything behind, I sold all I had and left for Switzerland. After a number of attempts, I managed to get a job in the organization. I took advantage of our common ethnicity and became a friend of his.

Two years later, I became his personal assistant. I was keeping his appointments, scribble his notes and fulfill all his desires. The thing was that I could be with him in his lab, looking at the machine he had created, coming to life. I watched the first experiments, with my mouth dry, waiting to see the results. I was there when he sent a puppy ten minutes in the past. I persuaded him to send it deeper, he did. The machine was functional.

Based on his notes, I learned how to send myself back in time. I have already configured the parameters. I will stay in 1999 for half an hour and then, I will return. I'm into the transfer cage, waiting. I hear the mechanisms work and close my eyes, am so close. Seconds later, I find myself in the sea. I am back. I can see the ship in front of me. I start screaming and moving my hands.

They see me. People are gathering on the railings, looking at me. High above my head, on the last deck, I can see my daughter. She stands next to my younger self. She is beautiful, alive and away from the cursed table we were sitting. They are tossing lifejackets to me. The ship turns around and they pull me on the catapult. It will soon be heard. There is the explosion. I'm standing up. Panic explodes. They forget all about me. I can hardly climb the stairs because the boat is dancing in the sea. I reach the deck. I can see myself holding her arms. She lifts her head and looks into my younger self's eyes. She is alive. She is ok.

I feel a pull deep in my guts and suddenly, I'm back in the lab. Outside the cage, my friend and boss is waiting for me.

"What have you done?" He screams as I walk out of the cage.

I try to explain and he bursts to tears.

"You cannot change the course of things," he says. "Time will find the way to complete itself. The order will be restored".

My legs bend and I sit on the floor. I hide my face in my hands and cry all the tears I never cried since the day I lost her. I am losing her again. I feel my heart stopping. I cannot take a breath.

"I am coming to you my love; I am finally coming to you".

Saturday, June 17, 1999

This morning and while we were ready to live the hospital, my daughter was moved to the intensive care. The doctors said that she has some kind of damage at her brain cortex, probably from the explosion. They said that they couldn't find it before. At two o'clock, she died. I am losing my mind. I want to ask God to take me and let her live. I don't care where He'll send me. After the funeral, I went to her mother's house. She called me a murderer. She said that it was my fault that the child was lost.

"I know", I answered. And with my eyes not even daring to cry, I left her home...

Short Story 10: Gülek's Pine Tree

That tree stands there for years, no one knows how many for sure. I remember that it was always the meeting point of our village. When we were kids, the pine was the place we would gather, riding our bikes after school, to start playing. In puberty, the pine was the place to rendezvous with our girls. Even today, when a stranger comes to our village, Gülek's pine is the central point of reference.

The odd thing, however, is that I do not remember having ever seen anyone touching that tree. Neither have I, I think. The more I think about it, the more certain I become. It's like there's something that drives you away, prevents you, forbidding you to touch it. It looks like it has a strange aura around it that does not even allow birds to stand on it to take a breath.

As far as its name is concerned, I'm not a hundred percent sure, but I remember a story, a tale my grandmother used to say about the era of the Ottoman domination. At that time, the Turkish lord of the area was Gülek Pasha. He was born of a Greek family from his mother's side, but had a Turkish father, and he was more of a Turk than the actual Turks.

Those times were hard and wild. It had nothing to do with ethnicity; it had to do with a man's soul. When a man, Greek or Turkish, had a black heart, like Gülek and at the same time had power, then everything was possible. As long as Gülek was ok to the empire, he was not controlled by anyone. The lives of the villagers really belonged to him.

My grandmother used to say that when he was passing in front of the pine on his way to his saray, he would hang on it, anyone who would dare to raise his eyes on him. That's probably why they call it "Gülek's pine". His mother, a daughter of our village, died out of sorrow. The fact that she saw her son growing up and becoming the monster he became, destroyed her. Eventually, she dived in the river and drowned, leaving Gülek crying like a kid, over her dead body.

Gülek also had a cousin from his mother' side, whom he hated but could not kill because he was a Christian priest. His death would cause the villagers to rebelliate. The Vizier's instructions were simple.

"Let the Greeks go to their churches as long as they are quiet and threaten them to ruin them when they start causing problems".

This, on one hand, was good for him, because he could keep the villagers happy, but on the other hand, his relation with Papa-Giannis, reminded him of his Greek ancestors.

Papa-Giannis, for his part, was both a priest and a teacher. He was helping the villagers to keep their religion alive, as well as their language and traditions. As soon as the congregation was over, he would keep the kids, talking to them about the ancient Greeks and Jesus Christ. He embraced religion with ancient Greece and made children's minds dream of hero-saints and holy heroes. He was filling the Greek children's hurts with pride for their enslaved country and religion. He would return to his home, late at night, just to catch a couple of hours of sleep.

Gülek knew it. He had a lot of people telling him everything happening in the village, so he was looking for a way to get rid of the young priest, without causing any problems with the rest of the village. Among the people he had in his house was Masaf, an Arab eunuch. He was his wife's personal servant, but clever enough to become the personal advisor of Gülek Pasha.

An afternoon Pasha was sitting in his garden and thinking of a way to get rid of his cousin, when the eunuch leaning until his nose, touched on the floor and told him:

"My lord, my Pasha, why don't you tell people the truth, since you know that the priest is not a Christian, he believes in the gods of the ancients and teaches that to their children?"

Gülek turned and looked at him with confusion written all over his face.

"What? How on earth can you even say that?"

The eunuch raised his body a little higher and, with a sly smile, he said to the Pasha:

"My pasha, I am not saying anything. You on the other hand, as his cousin, know better than everyone in what the priest believes. You are the Pasha, you are his cousin, who will deny the truth of your words?"

Gülek began to understand the meaning of Masaf's words. He smiled and summoned the captain of his guard.

"Tomorrow morning", he said, "while the priest will be in the church, you will go to his house and paint all the icons of saints. Then, you will put all the ancient Greek statues the priest has on a table and you will make it look like a place of prayer." The captain of the guard leaned his body in a sign of respect and left.

The next morning, when the job of the guard captain ended, Gülek took some of his soldiers and went down to the church. He stood outside and waited for the villagers to come out. When the villagers came out of the temple and saw Pasha, froze. In front of them, Papa-Giannis took a courageous step and asked Gülek what on earth was he doing outside their church.

Gülek, explained to the villagers, that as their pasha, even though he did not believe in the same God, he had to tell them about the satan they had among them. He told them that the priest is everything but a priest and that he teaches their children to believe in the ancient gods and not their Christ. After a while a lot of voices rose, but Gülek stopped them and asked if anybody had ever gone inside the priest's house. The villagers looked at each other. Of course they had never been there. Papa-Giannis was all day long in the church.

Gülek smiled tenderly, as a father confronted with the mischief of his children, and told them to send someone to look inside the priest's house. A young lad walked forward and said that he and his father would go. Gülek agreed and went and sat under the pine tree. He sat with his back on the tree and looked at his cousin, who seemed totally confused. He could not understand why the Pasha had sent people to his home.

After half an hour, father and son appeared returning from the end of the street, talking to each other wildly, holding something in their hands. As soon as they reached the priest, the young man struck him on his head, throwing him to the ground. The priest with blood flowing all over his face looked at Gülek who was smiling. He understood that he had been trapped.

After a while, the words of those who had seen his home created a storm. His fellow-villagers themselves, the people he adored and took care as if they were his own children, had hanged a rope from the pine tree, putting the loop around his neck. Gülek told them to wait and stood in front of him.

"We are cousins", he said, bent over and kissed him on his forehead.

The priest looked at his fellow villagers smiling and told them he did not consider them responsible for anything, he said good-bye to them and turned to Gülek.

"Judah of thy race and thy god, thou shalt die in this tree, alone, as thy mother also died because of thee. No one will touch you again, as she did not after her death. Goodbye my cousin, may His curse be with you."

Gülek took a step back, as if he had been slapped, and signaled to his soldiers to hang the priest. He gave him a last look and then, with a frozen face, he took the road to his saray.

Later the same night, in his sleep, he heard his mother's voice.

"Giannaki, Gülek, where are you? Why have you left me alone? I'm wet and I'm cold…"

Gülek, whose Greek name was Giannis, like his dead cousin, was jumped out, off his bed. With sweat flowing all over his body, he began to search all over his saray to find his mother.

Her voice was coming from the garden. Gülek, barefoot and wearing only his long underwear, came out to the courtyard.

"Sweet mother of mine, where are you? I am coming for you".

Following his mother's voice, he stepped into the street and began to walk towards the village, hurting his feet on the stones and thorns. His mother's voice sounded louder as he saw the church's bell tower. Gülek started running, crying.

"My mother, my sweet mother", his voice sounded, "Giannakis is coming to you. I will never let you alone again."

Arriving in front of the pine tree, he saw the body of his cousin hanging; nobody had even tried to take him down. On top of him, on the fork the rope that took his life was fastened, was his mother.

"My Giannaki", she said, "your cousin is here, but he can't help me" and showed him the priest's dead body.

"He cannot help you mother and am to blame for".

Gülek touched the priest's bearded cheek with love and then looked at his mother.

"I am here mother, I'll help you myself. I'll take you down and then, we'll go home."

He stepped on the roots of the pine tree and grabbed the rope his cousin was hanging from. He pulled his body upward and passed his head through the fork of the trunks.

"I am here mother" he said, "I am here."

At the same time, the rope that could not keep the weight of both men broke, and Gülek lost his balance and sled down. His neck was caught in the fork and broke, leaving his body hanging next to his cousin's body.

The morning of next day, the villagers were all wondering why Pasha's body was hanging next to their old priest's. A few hours later, they learned that the Pasha's eunuch would temporarily take his place. Something felt awfully wrong and no one ever touched Gülek's pine again.

About James Antoniou

James Antoniou is an author and translator. His great love is fiction as he likes to create worlds in which the reader can be lost and escape from the problems of his everyday life.

"I am trying to offer people around me everything the books offer to me. For me, a good book is companionship, a journey, the start and the end of my day."

James Antoniou has studied English Literature and Psychology, as well as Creative Writing. He has been writing for many years, working in his home place Greece and internationally. The author has three books published in Greece.

Essentially, his main kind of writing is somewhere between thriller and the "adult fairy-tale", as he likes to call it. However, he has so far dealt with other genres such as classical literature, steampunk and lastly, with detective adventures.

His personal view:

"Writers take partly the role of grandfather before the fireplace, when in the cold nights of winter walk their grandchildren in worlds where dragons, knights, witches and evil creatures are living."

Connect with James Antoniou

Writing stories has no value at all, if you do not have a circle of people around you to enjoy them. Words lose their meaning and dissolve in the winds of oblivion. So, welcome to our circle. Please, send me your comments and suggestions.

Subscribe to my personal blog (in English):

http://jamesantoniouofficial.blogspot.com/

And to get to know you better and create even more beautiful stories, I'm waiting for your e-mails at:

james.d.antoniou@gmail.com

Friend me on Facebook:

https://www.facebook.com/james.antoniou.798

Follow me on Twitter:

https://twitter.com/JamesDAntoniou

Follow me on GooglePlus:

https://plus.google.com/+JamesAntoniou

Follow me on Instagram:

https://www.instagram.com/james.d.antoniou/

Follow me on Pinterest:

https://gr.pinterest.com/jamesdantoniou/

Subscribe to my YouTube channel:

https://www.youtube.com/channel/UCiftpX2tdBAsdXxKgMNBkBQ?view_as=subscriber%3Fsub_confirr

Favorite me at Smashwords:

https://www.smashwords.com/profile/view/JamesAntoniou

James Antoniou
2nd Special Edition
Copyright 2021 James Antoniou
eCult Hub[1] Publications
Editing and Cover design by Anastasia Tsekeri

[2]

---

1. https://eculthub.blogspot.com/

2. https://eculthub.blogspot.com/

About the Author

James Antoniou is a writer and translator born in Greece, who studied English Literature, Psychology and Creative Writing. The author has been working both in his native country Greece, as well as internationally. His great love is fiction as he likes to create worlds in which the reader can get lost, in order to escape from the problems of his everyday life.The author's passion is adult fairytales, stories that according to him, is somewhat of a fairytale for kids transformed into something scarier, more grotesque and harsh. His personal point of view is that: "Writers are partly taking on the role of a grandfather in front of a fireplace, who in the cold nights of winter, walk their grandchildren into worlds with dragons, knights, witches, murderers and evil creatures."*******O James Antoniou είναι συγγραφέας και μεταφραστής. Η μεγάλη του αγάπη είναι η μυθοπλασία, καθώς του αρέσει να δημιουργεί κόσμους στους οποίους μπορεί να χαθεί ο αναγνώστης για να ξεφύγει από τα προβλήματα της καθημερινότητάς του.«Προσπαθώ δηλαδή να προσφέρω στους ανθρώπους γύρω μου, ό,τι προσφέρουν σε μένα τα βιβλία. Για μένα, ένα καλό βιβλίο είναι η συντροφιά, το ταξίδι, το ξεκίνημα και το τέλος της ημέρας.»Ο James Antoniou έχει σπουδάσει Αγγλική Φιλολογία και Ψυχολογία, καθώς και δημιουργική γραφή. Με την συγγραφή ασχολείται εδώ και πολλά χρόνια, δραστηριοποιούμενος και στη γενέτειρά του, την Ελλάδα, αλλά και σε διεθνές επίπεδο.Μέσα από διάφορες συνεργασίες, συμμετέχει σε αξιόλογες προσπάθειες στον ελληνικό χώρο, όπως για παράδειγμα η συμμετοχή του στις «Όψεις του Φανταστικού - Larry Niven» από τις εκδόσεις Συμπαντικές Διαδρομές, καθώς και κάποιες δικές του μεταφράσεις βιβλίων άλλων συγγραφέων. Ανάλογες συνεργασίες γίνονται και σε διεθνές επίπεδο, όπως η συμμετοχή του στην ανθολογία του «the Power of Friendship through Art».Στο παρελθόν, έχει παρουσιάσει κάποια ανέκδοτα βιβλία του στα ελληνικά, σε συνεργασία με διάφορους φορείς όπως το φεστιβάλ «Revault Open September Festival» του VAULT, και έχει κάνει μεταφορά ενός από τα πρώτα του βιβλία σε σενάριο, του βιβλίου «Αθάνατη Πραγματικότητα».Εκτός από τα βιβλία, έχει ασχοληθεί και με τη συγγραφή μια σειράς ερευνών, οι οποίες έδωσαν σε μεγάλο βαθμό και υλικό για τα βιβλία του, καθώς και με τη συγγραφή ιστοριών τύπου flash story, δοκιμίων, αστυνομικών σειρών, κ.α.Ουσιαστικά, το βασικό του είδος συγγραφής βρίσκεται κάπου ανάμεσα στο θρίλερ και το «παραμύθ...

Read more at https://jamesantoniouofficial.blogspot.com/.